Zach Hangs In There

William Mulcahy

illustrated by
Darren McKee

free spirit
PUBLISHING®

Library of Congress Cataloging-in-Publication Data
Names: Mulcahy, William, author. | McKee, Darren, illustrator.
Title: Zach hangs in there / William Mulcahy ; illustrated by Darren McKee.
Description: Minneapolis : Free Spirit Publishing, 2017. | Series: Zach rules series | Audience: Age: 5–8.
Identifiers: LCCN 2016034106 (print) | LCCN 2017005177 (ebook) | ISBN 9781631981623 (hardback) | ISBN 1631981625 (hardcover) |
   ISBN 9781631981630 (Web PDF) | ISBN 9781631981647 (ePub)
Subjects: LCSH: Goal (Psychology)—Juvenile literature. | Self-esteem—Juvenile literature. | BISAC: JUVENILE FICTION / Social Issues / Self-Esteem &
   Self-Reliance. | JUVENILE FICTION / Social Issues / Friendship. | JUVENILE FICTION / Social Issues / Emotions & Feelings.
Classification: LCC BF505.G6 M85 2017 (print) | LCC BF505.G6 (ebook) | DDC 158.1083—dc23
LC record available at https://lccn.loc.gov/2016034106

Free Spirit Publishing does not have control over or assume responsibility for author or third-party websites and their content.

Reading Level Grade 2; Interest Level Ages 5–8;
Fountas & Pinnell Guided Reading Level M

Edited by Eric Braun
Cover and interior design by Tasha Kenyon

10 9 8 7 6 5 4 3 2 1
Printed in the United States of America
B10950217

Free Spirit Publishing Inc.
6325 Sandburg Road, Suite 100
Minneapolis, MN 55427-3674
(612) 338-2068
help4kids@freespirit.com
www.freespirit.com

SUSTAINABLE FORESTRY INITIATIVE
Certified Chain of Custody
Promoting Sustainable Forestry
www.sfiprogram.org
SFI-01268

SFI label applies to the text stock

Free Spirit offers competitive pricing.
Contact edsales@freespirit.com for pricing information on multiple quantity purchases.

Dedication

To Kegen, Makenna, and Masen.
Never forget: Life and love are extraordinary. Hang in there.

Acknowledgments

Thank you once again to Eric Braun, master editor and occasional mind reader.

For ideas on the makeup of persevering, thank you to Rebecca Toetz, principal at Cushing Elementary, and Kelli Lewis.

For the endless nourishment I have received through the years while working there on my stories and my life, thank you to Rochester Deli.

To the rest of the crew that circulates ideas and images in my heart and mind at home: Thank you, Liam, Luke, and Jack.

Lastly, I am thankful for Melissa, for the great gift of parenthood, and for our newest addition. Welcome, Shannon Helen.

Zach finished his math test and handed it in to Ms. Rosamond. It was almost time for recess. He started thinking about those tricky trapeze rings.

Zach went out to recess with his best friend, Sonya.

"Are you going to the trapeze rings again?" Sonya asked. Lately they had been going there every recess.

"I have to get across them," Zach said.

"Why do you care so much, anyway?" Sonya asked.

Zach thought about that. "I don't know," he said. "I just do. Those rings are so hard for me. It will feel really good to get across them."

But when they got to the rings, Zach didn't move.

"What's the matter?" Sonya asked.

"I'm not sure I can do it."

"Sure you can," Sonya said.

"Easy for you to say," Zach said. "You already **can** do the trapeze rings."

5

"I couldn't always do them," Sonya said. "It took me a lot of tries. Do you know what your plan is?"

Zach climbed up to the platform. "My plan is to try not to look stupid."

"No, I'm serious," Sonya said. "My dad says when I try something hard it helps to have a plan."

Zach had never really thought of having a plan. He just wanted to get across without falling. Then he got an idea. "My plan is to go across as fast as I can before my arms get tired."

Zach jumped for the first ring and grabbed it. As he lunged for the second ring, his fingers slipped and he fell to the ground.

"Aargh!" Zach yelled. "I am so done with these rings!"

"But you almost made it," Sonya said.

"What planet are you on?" Zach said.

The word planet gave Sonya an idea. "Do you remember last week when we were playing Robo Rocket Quest? You didn't give up no matter how hard it was. You made it to Planet Level 12. That's higher than anyone I know."

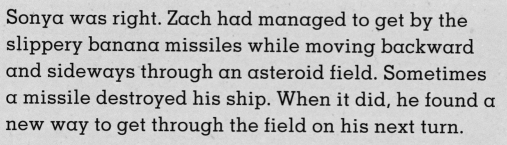

Sonya was right. Zach had managed to get by the slippery banana missiles while moving backward and sideways through an asteroid field. Sometimes a missile destroyed his ship. When it did, he found a new way to get through the field on his next turn.

Zach said, "I've got to come up with a new way to do the trapeze rings. My way doesn't work. How do **you** do them?"

Sonya shrugged. "It's hard to explain. Here, I'll show you."

Sonya grabbed the first ring and swung back and forth to get closer to the next ring. She made it all the way across.

"Wow," Zach said. "You're good."

"Thanks. It took me a long time to get it."

"I think I have an idea," Zach said.

He climbed onto the platform and reached out for the first ring. This time, he rocked back and forth. As he swung forward, the second ring was easier to reach than ever before. He tried to rock to the third bar, but his arms ached too much. He let go and fell to the ground.

"Great job!" said Sonya. "You got farther than before."

"I'm going to try again," Zach said.

"You can do it, Zach. Don't give up!"

His good friend's words gave Zach confidence. The words "You can do it," and "Don't give up" repeated in his head as he climbed the platform to try again.

He reached out for the first ring and swung back. When he swung forward, he grabbed the second bar tightly, feeling its cold metal against his hand.

"You can do it, don't give up," he said to himself.

He swung out and grabbed the third bar. His arms ached, but he didn't let go. One more ring.

You can do it. Don't give up.

He swung and grabbed the last ring. Then he swung onto the other platform.

15

"You did it!" Sonya yelled.

Zach jumped off the platform and gave her a high five. "Thanks for your help!" he said.

Zach felt great. Sometimes he'd worried he would never make it across the trapeze rings. But he didn't give up, and his hard work paid off.

Their teacher, Ms. Rosamond came over to see what was going on. "What's all the excitement about?" she asked.

Sonya told her what Zach had done.

Ms. Rosamond said, "Congratulations, Zach. It sounds like you achieved a goal that was important to you. Having a goal is the first step to achieving something hard. What other steps did you do?"

"Sonya had the idea for the next step," Zach said. "Make a plan."

"It was my dad's idea really," Sonya said.

"Well it's a good one," Ms. Rosamond said. "What came next?"

The two kids looked at each other trying to remember. "We talked about a video game," Sonya said.

"Oh yeah," Zach said. "When I was playing Robo Rocket Quest, I found a new way to get past the hard part when my first idea didn't work."

Sonya said, "And when you watched me go across, you figured out a new way to try it."

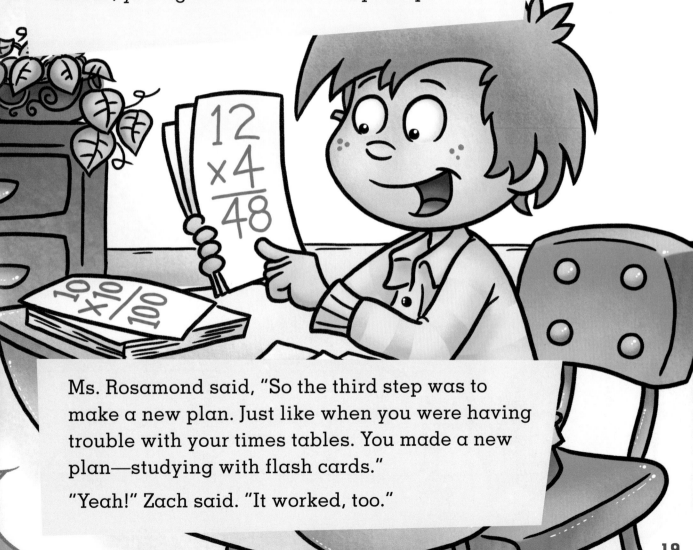

Ms. Rosamond said, "So the third step was to make a new plan. Just like when you were having trouble with your times tables. You made a new plan—studying with flash cards."

"Yeah!" Zach said. "It worked, too."

"Did you have any more steps?" Ms. Rosamond asked.

Zach shrugged. "Just keep trying," he said.

WALL OF FAME

"Did anything help you keep trying?"

"Well," Zach said, "it's kind of silly. I kept saying, **You can do it. Don't give up.** Over and over."

"That's not silly at all," Ms. Rosamond said. "It's called **positive self-talk**. When you give yourself positive messages, it really helps you keep going."

$2 \times 12 = 24$

"It **did** seem to help," Zach said.

"The way you two figured this out really worked," Ms. Rosamond said. "It could help you again. How can you remember those steps for next time?"

21

"Hey," Sonya said. "There are four steps just like there are four rings! Maybe we could use the rings as a tool. The Hang-In-There Rings!"

"Awesome!" Zach said.

Sonya drew four rings on a sheet of paper. In the first ring, Zach wrote the words, **Start with a goal.** In the second ring, he wrote, **Make a plan.** He wrote, **Make a new plan if you need it** in the third ring. He labeled the fourth ring with, **Keep trying to the end.**

When they were done, Sonya and Zach asked Ms. Rosamond to take a picture of them with their new tool to remember what they accomplished.

To help you learn how to hang in there when you feel like giving up, you can use Zach and Sonya's **Hang-In-There Rings**. In the first ring, write what you want to do and why it's important to you. In the second ring, write how you're going to meet your goal. Write a new plan in the third ring if your first way isn't working. And in the last ring, write some ideas that will help you keep going until the end. You can write some positive self-talk ideas, such as "Believe," "Don't give up," or "You can do it." Finishing what you started can help you feel better about yourself and what you are doing.

Helping Children Persevere

Perseverance, or the ability to keep trying even when something is difficult, is by its nature challenging for both kids and adults. For some of us, it is much easier to give up. While most adults have the skills and experience to persevere during difficult times, young children typically need coaching and support to hang in there and keep trying until a task is completed.

It's important to remember that all children have had their own experiences with perseverance before the present learning situation. Some children tend to handle challenges with a fierce determination, becoming intensely focused on accomplishing things. Others are easily discouraged, displaying avoidance, emotional outbursts, complaints, or other behavioral issues. Most children fall somewhere in between, having experienced the benefits and woes of persevering. In any case, children will carry that emotional and behavioral history into the current potential learning situation. The Hang-In-There Rings can empower all children to take an active role in their learning and success, providing a road map to work through the struggles, doubt, and emotional upheaval that often surface while facing obstacles.

The Hang-In-There Rings comprise a four-step process that not only helps kids get through the challenge they are facing, but also better prepares them for challenges in the future. It gently shows children how persevering can become an "everyday-everyway" habit.

The Hang-In-There Rings are most successful when children and adults partner in learning and practicing the steps. It is vital that adults offer children reassurances and encouragement and be willing to support them with an eye to gradually lessening that support so that children become independent in using the rings—and ultimately in trying new things and learning.

The Hang-In-There Rings have the power to:

- Provide clear guidance on how to stick with it through tough times
- Build confidence
- Help kids distinguish between ideas that work and those that don't work
- Help kids learn responsibility and feel empowered
- Foster autonomy and a sense of accomplishment
- Improve positive self-talk
- Help kids make constructive choices
- Help us all understand the importance of the journey as well as the end goal

Here is more information about the four steps of the Hang-In-There Rings and some tips to help guide your child:

1. **Start with a goal.** In this step, children identify what they are trying to accomplish and why it's important. Insist that kids make clear to themselves—specifically— what they are shooting for. Don't be afraid to push them to answer why the task is important to them. How will they feel when they finish? What will be different for them? If they don't know what their goal is, they can stumble around aimlessly wasting time and energy and setting themselves up for failure. The type of forward-thinking needed to set a goal and know why it's important is essential in helping children grow into critical thinkers and dynamic learners.

2. **Make a plan.** Here, children take an active role in piecing together a viable plan that will allow them to accomplish their goal. Encourage them to analyze a problem or situation and develop a system or a way to attack the task at hand. Feedback and directions from adults can be a powerful coaching tool during this step, but be sure you are *supporting* as children develop their own abilities to analyze problems and construct plans to achieve goals.

3. **Make a new plan if you need it.** Sometimes your first plan doesn't work. When that happens, children review and revise the strategies they have been using. One of the vital ingredients in this step is helping kids develop the awareness that something isn't working and give themselves permission to try something new. Proactively encourage and coach kids to brainstorm new tactics and develop more problem-solving strategies. Don't forget to give them the needed time to sift through the possible solutions for accomplishing their goals.

4. **Keep trying to the end.** In this step, children learn how to keep trying until their task is accomplished. Teach kids to visualize themselves working through the difficult moments *all the way to the end*. Teach children positive self-talk to assist themselves as they are attempting to persevere. Phrases such as "Don't give up," "I can do it," and "Believe" are powerful prompts to continue even when things get hard. Don't forget to encourage children to examine how they accomplished what they set out to do and appropriately celebrate their efforts and achievement.

A few other tips:

- Never punish, intimidate, or shame a child for struggling with a task or for giving up. The line between being encouraging and being demanding is not always clear. A general rule of thumb is to make sure you keep a child's dignity intact.

- The language that adults use impacts how children think about themselves. It is important to use language that supports learning and growth. Focus on effort, and be specific. For instance, instead of saying, "You did a good job," use phrases such as, "You worked really hard on the violin today," or "I love the creative way you practiced your spelling words."

- Applaud effort, not perfection.

- When introducing new or difficult tasks, avoid phrases such as, "This is really easy," which can be frustrating for kids. If it was easy, they wouldn't have to persevere! Instead, explain the task patiently and encourage them: "You can do it." "I'm here to help."

- While it is important to stress with children to never give up and to finish what they started, there are times when giving up is healthy and appropriate. For instance, the child who chooses an unrealistic goal may need support in rethinking the goal. In these situations, it's entirely appropriate to give up and try something else.

During their lives, children will experience many situations in which they will need to persevere. When we believe in children's ability to achieve, we help them build the skills and tenacity to do so. Use the Hang-In-There Rings to support children on their journey and in accomplishing their goals.

Download a printable copy of the Hang-In-There Rings at www.freespirit.com/goal.

About the Author

William Mulcahy is a licensed professional counselor and psychotherapist. He has served as supervisor at Family Service of Waukesha and as a counselor at Stillwaters Cancer Support Center in Wisconsin, specializing in grief and cancer-related issues, and he has worked with children with special needs. Currently he works in private practice in Pewaukee, Wisconsin, and he is the owner of Kids Cope Now, a program for providing books and tools to help kids better cope with life's difficulties. Bill's picture books include the Zach Rules series and *Zoey Goes to the Hospital*. He lives in Summit, Wisconsin, with four children, three stepchildren, and his wife Melissa in a home where life is never boring. His website is kidscopenow.com.

About the Illustrator

Darren McKee has illustrated books for many publishers over his 20-year career. When not working, he spends his time riding his bike, reading, drawing, and traveling. He lives in Dallas, Texas, with his wife Debbie.

More Great Books from Free Spirit

Zach Rules Series

by William Mulcahy, illustrated by Darren McKee

Zach struggles with social issues like getting along, persevering, handling frustrations, making mistakes, and other everyday problems typical of young kids. Each book in the Zach Rules series presents a single, simple storyline involving one such problem. As each story develops, Zach and readers learn straightforward tools for coping with their struggles and building stronger relationships now and in the future.

Each book: 32 pp., color illust., HC, 8¼" x 8¼", ages 5–8.

Penelope Perfect
A Tale of Perfectionism Gone Wild
by Shannon Anderson, illustrated by Katie Kath

48 pp., color illust., PB & HC, 8" x 10", ages 5–9.

Coasting Casey
A Tale of Busting Boredom in School
by Shannon Anderson, illustrated by Colleen Madden

48 pp., color illust., PB & HC, 8" x 10", ages 5–9.

Interested in purchasing multiple quantities and receiving volume discounts?
Contact edsales@freespirit.com or call 1.800.735.7323 and ask for Education Sales.

Many Free Spirit authors are available for speaking engagements, workshops, and keynotes.
Contact speakers@freespirit.com or call 1.800.735.7323.

For pricing information, to place an order, or to request a free catalog, contact:

free spirit PUBLISHING®

6325 Sandburg Road • Suite 100 • Minneapolis, MN 55427-3674
toll-free 800.735.7323 • local 612.338.2068 • fax 612.337.5050
help4kids@freespirit.com • www.freespirit.com